# GEORGE AND MARTHA RISE AND SHINE

# For My Father

The stories in this book were originally published by
Houghton Mifflin Company in *George and Martha: Rise and Shine,* 1976.

Houghton Mifflin Books for Children is an imprint of Houghton Mifflin
Harcourt Publishing Company.

www.hmhbooks.com

*Library of Congress Cataloging-in-Publication Data is on file.*
ISBN-13: 978-0-547-14425-2

Printed in Singapore

TWP 10 9 8 7 6 5 4 3 2 1

# GEORGE AND MARTHA RISE AND SHINE

*written and illustrated by*

JAMES MARSHALL

HOUGHTON MIFFLIN BOOKS FOR CHILDREN
HOUGHTON MIFFLIN HARCOURT
BOSTON • NEW YORK • 2009

# THREE STORIES ABOUT TWO FINE FRIENDS

~

# STORY NUMBER ONE

# THE FIBBER

One day George wanted to impress Martha.

"I used to be a champion jumper," he said.

Martha raised an eyebrow.

"And," said George, "I used to be a wicked pirate."

"Hmmm," said Martha.

George tried harder. "Once I was even a famous snake charmer!"

"Oh, goody," said Martha.

7

Martha went to the closet and got out Sam.

"Here's a snake for you to charm."

"Eeeek," cried George.

And he jumped right out of his chair.

"It's only a toy *stuffed* snake," said Martha. "I'm surprised a famous snake charmer is such a scaredy-cat."

"I told some fibs," said George.

"For shame," said Martha.

"But you can see what a good jumper I am," said George.

"That's true," said Martha.

# STORY NUMBER TWO

# THE EXPERIMENT

Martha was in her laboratory.

"What are you doing?" asked George.

"I'm studying fleas," said Martha.

"Cute little critters," said George.

"You don't understand," said Martha.

"This is serious. This is science."

The next day, George noticed that Martha was scratching a lot. She looked uncomfortable.

George bought Martha some special soap.

After her shower Martha felt much better.

"I think I'll stop studying fleas," said Martha.

"Good idea," said George.

"I think I'll study bees instead," said Martha.

"Oh dear," said George.

# STORY NUMBER
# 3

# THE Picnic

One Saturday morning, George wanted
to sleep late.
"I love sleeping late," said George.
But Martha had other ideas.
She wanted to go on a picnic.
"Here she comes!" said George to himself.

Martha did her best to get George out of bed.

"Picnic time!" sang Martha.

But George didn't budge.

Martha played a tune on her saxophone.

George put little balls of cotton in his ears
and pulled up the covers.

Martha tickled George's toes.

"Stop it!" said George.

"Picnic time!" sang Martha.

"But I'm *not* going on a picnic!" said George.

"Oh yes you *are!*" said his friend.

Martha had a clever idea.

"This is such hard work," she said, huffing and puffing.

"But I'm not going to help," said George.

"I'm getting tired," said Martha.

George had fun on the picnic.

"I'm so glad we came," said George.

But Martha wasn't listening.

She had fallen asleep.

JAMES MARSHALL (1942–1992) is one of the most popular and celebrated artists in the field of children's literature. Three of his books were selected as New York Times Best Illustrated Books, and he received a Caldecott Honor Award in 1989 for *Goldilocks and the Three Bears*. With more than seventy-five books to his credit, including the popular George and Martha series, Marshall has earned the admiration and love of countless readers.